ANNE OF
GREEN GABLES

W9-CGO-637

Library of Congress Cataloging-in-Publication Data

Mattern, Joanne, (date)
 Anne of Green Gables / by L.M. Montgomery; retold by Joanne
Mattern; illustrated by Renee Graef.
  p.   cm.
 Summary: Anne, an eleven-year-old orphan, is sent by mistake to
live with a lonely, middle-aged brother and sister on a Prince
Edward Island farm and proceeds to make an indelible impression on
everyone around her.
 ISBN 0-8167-2866-6 (lib. bdg.)   ISBN 0-8167-2867-4 (pbk.)
 [1. Orphans—Fiction. 2. Friendship—Fiction. 3. Country life—
Fiction. 4. Prince Edward Island—Fiction.] I. Montgomery, L.M.
(Lucy Maud), 1874-1942. II. Graef, Renee, ill. III. Title.
PZ7.M43165An 1993
[Fic]—dc20   92-12703

Copyright © 1993 by Troll Associates.

Illustrations copyright © 1993 by Renee Graef.

All rights reserved. No portion of this book may be
reproduced in any form, electronic or mechanical,
including photocopying, recording, or information
storage and retrieval systems, without prior written
permission from the publisher.

Printed in the United States of America.
10 9 8 7 6 5 4 3 2 1

ANNE OF GREEN GABLES

L.M. MONTGOMERY

Retold by
Joanne Mattern

Illustrated by
Renee Graef

Troll Associates

Mrs. Rachel Lynde lived just where the Avonlea main road dipped into a little hollow, ringed all around with trees and flowers. Mrs. Lynde was very fond of sitting in her window and watching everyone's comings and goings. She was one of those people who could attend not only to her own business, but everyone else's as well.

One afternoon in early June, Mrs. Lynde was sitting in her usual spot, knitting a quilt in the warm sunshine that poured through the window. Suddenly, she received a great surprise. There was her neighbor, Matthew Cuthbert, driving his horse and buggy out of town, and wearing his best suit of clothes!

Mrs. Lynde could not imagine where Matthew could be going. He should have been sowing turnip seed on his farm. Besides, Matthew was the shyest man alive. He was not the type to go visiting, especially when there was work to do.

If Mrs. Lynde had known where Matthew Cuthbert was going that bright June day, she would have been even more surprised. For Matthew and his sister, Marilla, had decided to adopt a little orphan boy to help them with the work on their farm. Matthew was on his way to the railroad station to pick up the child.

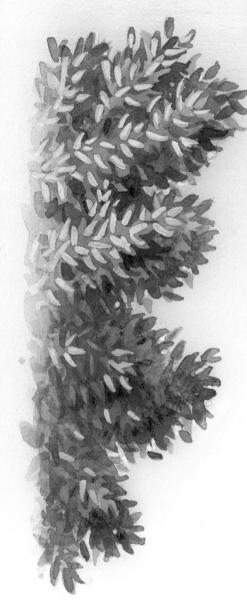

When Matthew reached the station, there wasn't a train in sight. Nor was there any little boy waiting for him. The only person he saw was a little girl sitting on the end of the platform. Matthew was very shy around strangers, especially girls, so he said nothing to her as he went into the station.

"When is the five-thirty train due?" Matthew asked the stationmaster.

"That train has been and gone already," the stationmaster told him. "But there was a passenger on it for you. A little girl. She's waiting for you outside."

"But I'm not expecting a girl!" said Matthew. "The orphanage was supposed to send me a boy."

"Maybe they were out of boys," the stationmaster joked. "All I know is there's a little girl outside waiting for you. Now I'm going home to have my supper."

Poor Matthew was left with nothing to do but ask a strange girl why she wasn't a boy. He groaned as he started down the platform.

The little girl watched Matthew as he shuffled toward her. As he came near, she stood up and held out her hand.

"I suppose you are Mr. Matthew Cuthbert of Green Gables?" she asked. "I am very glad to see you. I was afraid you weren't coming for me, and I was imagining all the terrible things that might have happened to you. I'm very good at imagining. I had just made up my mind that if you didn't come for me tonight, I would climb up into that big cherry tree and spend the night there. I wouldn't be a bit afraid. Don't you think it would be lovely to sleep in a wild cherry tree, with the moonlight shining all around? But I'm very glad you've come, even though I can't sleep in the cherry tree now."

Matthew looked at the scrawny child with the bright, glowing eyes. He simply could not tell her that there had been a mistake. He would take her home to Green Gables and let his sister, Marilla, tell her. She was better at that sort of thing than he was.

"I'm sorry I was late," he said shyly.

"Come along now."

The little girl chattered all the way home. Her talk made Matthew a bit dizzy, but he found himself enjoying her company. This little girl was not like the Avonlea children, who made Matthew nervous. He liked her chatter, and so he let her talk as much as she wanted to.

At last, they came to the crest of a hill. Matthew said, "We're pretty near home now. There's Green Gables."

The little girl stared in wonder down into the valley, which glowed in the mellow afterlight of sunset. Then her gaze traveled to the hills beyond, where snug farms nestled along the slope. Her eyes lingered on a house far back from the road, and she knew that was her new home.

"Listen to the trees talking in their sleep," the child whispered as Matthew drove the buggy into the yard. "What nice dreams they must have!"

Matthew, however, was uneasy. He knew that arrangements to send the child back to the orphanage would have to be made. He was very glad that this was Marilla's responsibility.

Marilla was waiting for them in the house. When her eyes fell on the little girl, she said in amazement, "Matthew Cuthbert, who's that? Where is the boy?"

"There wasn't any boy," Matthew said miserably. "There was only her."

The little girl suddenly understood what was going on. "You don't want me!" she cried. "Nobody has ever wanted me. I might have known this was all too beautiful to last." Then she burst into tears.

"There's no need to cry about it," Marilla said sternly.

"Yes, there is! You would cry, too, if you were an orphan and had come to a place you thought was going to be your home and then found out they didn't want you because you weren't a boy. Oh, this is the most tragical thing that's ever happened to me!"

Something like a reluctant smile spread slowly across Marilla's face. "Well, don't cry any more," she said. "We aren't going to turn you out of doors tonight. Now, what's your name?"

"Will you please call me Cordelia?" the child asked hopefully.

"*Call* you Cordelia? Is that your name?"

"No-o-o, but I'd love to be called that. It's such an elegant name."

"If Cordelia isn't your name, what is?"

"Anne Shirley," the little girl said reluctantly. "Anne spelled with an *e*. It looks so much nicer that way. If you'll only call me Anne spelled with an *e*, I shall try to reconcile myself to not being called Cordelia."

"Very well, Anne spelled with an *e*. Now, take off your hat and sit down to supper."

After Anne went to bed that night, Matthew and Marilla had a discussion. "Well, this is a pretty kettle of fish," Marilla said. "The girl will have to be sent back to the orphanage, of course."

"I suppose so," Matthew said reluctantly.

"You *suppose* so? You don't mean to tell me you think we should keep her?" Marilla demanded.

"Well now, she is a nice little thing," Matthew said. "It'd be a pity to send her back when she's so set on staying here."

"What good would she be to us?" Marilla asked sternly.

"We might be some good to her." Matthew looked thoughtfully at his sister. "I could hire a boy to help me with the farm, and Anne would be good company for you."

"I don't need any company," Marilla stated. "We're not keeping her, and that's final."

Matthew said nothing more.

The next day, Marilla asked Anne to tell her about herself. Anne said that she was eleven years old. Her parents had been teachers, and they had both died of a fever when she was only three months old. After that, Anne had lived with different neighbors, but none of them really wanted her. She'd spent most of her life taking care of people's children and working much harder than a little girl should. Finally, when no one else would take her in, she'd been sent to the orphanage.

Marilla felt sorry for the girl. It was clear that she'd never had a real home. She had never been loved. "What if I do what Matthew wants and let the girl stay?" Marilla asked herself. "She seems like a good girl, even if she does talk too much, and she certainly needs a home." She looked at Anne's pale face and sad eyes and felt that if she sent the child back, that face would haunt her for the rest of her life.

"You may stay at Green Gables," Marilla said at last, "if you're a good girl, of course. Why, child, what's the matter?" For Anne had burst into tears.

"I'm crying for joy," Anne told her.

The days passed, and Anne made herself quite at home at Green Gables. She loved playing in the woods, and spent every spare minute in the orchard or down by the brook. The trees and flowers became her closest friends.

One day, Mrs. Rachel Lynde came to visit. She was curious about the orphan girl, but had not had a chance to come to Green Gables to see her for herself. So she was happy to visit with Marilla, especially when her friend went to the door and called Anne inside.

Anne burst in, her bright red hair flying around her. ''Well, they didn't pick you for your looks, that's for sure,'' was the first thing Mrs. Lynde said. ''You're awful skinny and homely. Did anyone ever see such freckles! And hair as red as carrots!''

If there was one thing Anne did not like about herself, it was her red hair. ''I hate you!'' she screamed at Mrs. Lynde. ''How dare you call me ugly? You are a rude, unfeeling woman!''

''Anne!'' exclaimed Marilla.

''How would you feel if I said that you were fat and clumsy and hadn't a spark of imagination in you?'' Anne asked Mrs. Lynde in a fury. ''I hope I've hurt your feelings by saying so. You have hurt mine, and I'll *never* forgive you for it, never!''

''Anne, go to your room!'' Marilla commanded. Anne burst into tears and rushed upstairs.

"Well," Mrs. Lynde said, "I don't envy you bringing up a child like that!"

"You shouldn't have made fun of her looks," Marilla said, as much to her surprise as to Mrs. Lynde's. She knew that what Anne had done was wrong, but she could not help but agree with some of what the child had said.

After Mrs. Lynde had gone home, Marilla went upstairs and demanded that Anne apologize to Mrs. Lynde.

"I can never do that," said Anne. "You may punish me any way you like. You can shut me up in a dark, damp dungeon, and I won't complain. But I cannot ask Mrs. Lynde to forgive me."

"We're not in the habit of shutting people up in dungeons in Avonlea," Marilla responded. "You will apologize to Mrs. Lynde and that's final. Now, you're not to leave this room until you're ready to do what I've told you."

Anne stayed in her room that night and all of the next day. Marilla sent trays of food up to her, but Anne could not eat a bite. Matthew began to worry about her. Finally, when Marilla was outside that evening, he slipped up to Anne's room.

"Well now, Anne," he said awkwardly, "don't you think you'd better apologize to Mrs. Lynde and get it over with? Marilla's a dreadful determined woman, and she won't rest until you do as you're told."

"I suppose I could do it if it would make you happy," Anne said slowly. "I really am sorry now, and ashamed of myself for shouting at her. I made up my mind that I'd stay up here forever rather than embarrass myself by apologizing to Mrs. Lynde. But I'll do anything for you— if you really want me to."

"Well now, of course I do. It's awfully lonesome downstairs without you."

"Very well, I'll do it," Anne decided. When Marilla came inside, Anne told her she was willing to go see Mrs. Lynde.

When Anne and Marilla entered Mrs. Lynde's house, Anne fell to her knees. "Oh, Mrs. Lynde," she cried, "I am so terribly sorry! I could never express all my sorrow, not if I used up a whole dictionary. I behaved terribly to you, and I've disgraced Matthew and Marilla. Oh, please, please forgive me! If you refuse, it will be a lifelong sorrow to me. Please say you forgive me."

"There, there, get up, child," Mrs. Lynde said kindly. She was a bit overwhelmed by Anne's apology. "Of course I forgive you. I shouldn't have said those things in the first place, but that's just the way I am. Your hair *is* a terrible red—but I went to school with a girl whose hair was as red as yours, and when she grew up, it darkened to a real pretty shade. I wouldn't be surprised if yours did the same thing."

"Oh, Mrs. Lynde, you have given me hope!" Anne exclaimed as she got to her feet. "I could endure anything if I only thought my hair wouldn't be so red when I grew up."

As Anne and Marilla walked home that night, Anne said, "I apologized pretty well, didn't I? I thought since I had to do it, I might as well do it thoroughly."

"You did it thoroughly, right enough," was Marilla's answer. Anne's dramatic apology made her want to laugh, but Marilla would never admit that.

Summer passed. Anne became best friends with Diana Barry, a plump, dark-haired girl who lived nearby. The two spent the long days and evenings playing outside and imagining all sorts of adventures in the woods and fields. Diana was not a girl full of imagination, but Anne more than made up for her.

September came, and Diana and Anne headed off to school together. Marilla had been afraid that Anne wouldn't get along well with the other children, but she needn't have worried. Anne loved school, and she soon had many friends among the little girls there.

Several of the boys in school took notice of Anne as well. One of them was Gilbert Blythe. He tried everything to get Anne to notice him, but nothing seemed to work.

Gilbert was a handsome boy, and he wasn't used to having a girl ignore him. One day, when the teacher was working with one of the older students in the back of the room, Gilbert reached across the aisle and picked up the end of Anne's long red braid.

"Carrots!" Gilbert said in a loud whisper. "Carrots!"

Anne looked at him then! She jumped to her feet and glared at Gilbert with eyes that sparkled with both anger and tears.

"You mean, hateful boy!" she cried. "How dare you?" Then—

Thwack! Anne brought her slate down on Gilbert's head so hard that the slate cracked clear across.

$7 \times 6 = 42$
$7 \times 7 = 49$

$8 \times 3 = 24$

Everyone said "Oh!" in horrified delight. The teacher, Mr. Phillips, stalked down the aisle and laid his hand heavily on Anne's shoulder. "What is the meaning of this?" he demanded.

It was Gilbert who answered. "It was my fault, Mr. Phillips," he said. "I teased her."

Mr. Phillips paid no attention to him. "I am sorry to see a pupil of mine displaying such a temper," he said to Anne. "Go and stand in front of the blackboard for the rest of the afternoon."

Anne would have preferred a whipping to this public embarrassment, but she had no choice. Her face as white as a ghost's, she obeyed the teacher.

At last, school was dismissed. As Anne marched out with her red head held high, Gilbert caught up with her.

"I'm awful sorry I made fun of your hair, Anne," he said. "Don't be mad for keeps."

Anne swept past without any sign that she had heard him. "Oh, how could you, Anne?" whispered Diana as they walked home. She was sure she would not have been able to ignore handsome Gilbert.

"I shall never forgive Gilbert Blythe," said Anne firmly.

After that, Anne flung herself into her studies with new determination. She would not be outdone in any subject by Gilbert.

At the end of the term, both Anne and Gilbert were promoted to the fifth class. Now they would study Latin, geometry, French, and algebra—and continue to be rivals for the head of the class.

One February evening, Anne ran breathlessly into the house. She had just been outside talking to Diana.

"Marilla, guess what?" she said excitedly. "Tomorrow is Diana's birthday. Her mother told her she could ask me to spend the night at her house. And her cousins are going to a concert at the hall tomorrow night, and they've invited Diana and me to go along. You will let me go, won't you, Marilla?"

At first, Marilla said no. She did not approve of children going out at night and sleeping in strange beds. None of Anne's pleading would change her mind. But Matthew shyly insisted that Anne should go. Finally, Marilla agreed.

Anne grew ever more excited during school the next day. But the real excitement began after school, when Anne went home with Diana. The girls had a very elegant tea, then went up to Diana's room to dress and do their hair.

When Diana's cousins came, everyone crowded into their big sleigh, nestling into the straw and furry robes. The sleigh slipped along the satin-smooth roads with the snow crisping under the runners. Anne felt she had never been happier.

The concert itself was a delight from beginning to end. The choir sang and there were readings from some of the students at school. Anne listened intently to all but one. When Gilbert Blythe got up to recite, Anne opened a book—and read until he'd finished.

It was eleven o'clock when Anne and Diana got home. Everybody was asleep, and the house was dark and silent. The girls tiptoed into the parlor, heading toward the spare room at the far end.

''Let's undress here,'' Diana said, standing before the stove. ''It's so nice and warm.''

They slipped quickly into their night clothes. ''Let's run a race and see who gets into bed first,'' Anne suggested.

Diana thought this was a wonderful idea. The two girls flew down the long room, ran through the spare-room door, and bounded on the bed at the same moment. And then—someone moved beneath them!

"Merciful goodness!" someone cried from underneath the covers.

Anne and Diana were never able to tell just how they got off that bed and out of the room. The next thing they knew, they were tiptoeing upstairs.

"Who—what—was it?" whispered Anne, her teeth chattering with cold and fright.

"It was Aunt Josephine," said Diana, gasping with laughter. "She's Father's aunt. She's awfully old and very prim and proper. I don't believe she was ever a little girl. She'll be furious about this, but—did you ever know anything so funny?"

The girls ended up sleeping with Diana's little sister. Miss Josephine Barry did not appear at the breakfast table the next morning. So Anne did not know the results of their actions until late afternoon when she went to Mrs. Lynde's house on an errand.

"So you and Diana nearly frightened poor old Miss Barry to death last night," Mrs. Lynde said to her. "Diana's mother told me that Miss Barry was in a terrible temper this morning—and Josephine Barry's temper is no joke, I can tell you that. She won't speak to Diana at all."

"It wasn't Diana's fault," said Anne. "It was mine. I suggested racing to see who could get into bed first."

"I knew it!" said Mrs. Lynde. "Well, it's made a nice lot of trouble. Old Miss Barry came to stay for a month, but now she says she's going back to town tomorrow. And she was going to pay for music lessons for Diana, but she won't now."

Anne knew she had to set things right for Diana. She stopped by her friend's house on her way home. "I am going to tell your aunt that what happened last night was my fault," she announced to Diana.

Diana was astonished. "Anne Shirley, she'll eat you alive!" she said.

"Don't frighten me any more than I am already," Anne begged. "I've got to do it. It was my fault and I have to confess. I've had practice in confessing, fortunately."

With that, Anne walked up to the spare-room door and knocked. "Come in!" said a sharp voice.

Miss Josephine Barry was knitting by the fire, her eyes still snapping with anger. "Who are you?" she demanded.

"I'm Anne of Green Gables," Anne said nervously. "I've come to confess. It was all my fault about jumping into bed on you last night. I suggested it. Diana would never have thought of such a thing. She is a very ladylike girl. So you must see how unfair it is to blame her."

"Oh, I must, hey? I rather think Diana did her share of the jumping," Miss Barry said sternly.

"But we were only having fun," Anne insisted. "If you must be cross with anyone, be cross with me, and not Diana. I'm used to having people cross with me, and I can endure it much better than Diana can."

Much of the snap had gone out of the old lady's eyes by this time, and she was beginning to look amused. But she said, "I don't think it's any excuse for you that you were only having fun. You don't know what it is to be awakened out of a sound sleep by two girls bouncing down on you."

"No, I don't, but I can imagine it," said Anne. "And there is our side of it, too. We didn't know there was anybody in the bed, and you nearly scared us to death. Can you imagine how we felt?"

Miss Barry actually laughed. "I'm afraid my imagination is a little rusty," she said. "It's been so long since I've used it. I suppose your claim to sympathy is as good as mine. Sit down and tell me about yourself."

"I'm sorry, but I can't," said Anne. "I must go home to Miss Marilla Cuthbert. She is a very kind lady who has taken me in to bring up properly. She is doing her best, but it is very discouraging work. But before I go, I wish you would tell me if you are going to forgive Diana and stay in Avonlea for as long as you meant to."

"I think perhaps I will, if you will come over and talk to me occasionally," said Miss Barry.

That evening, Miss Barry gave Diana a silver bangle bracelet and told the family that she had unpacked her suitcase. "I've made up my mind to stay only because of that Anne-girl," she said. "She amuses me, and at my age, an amusing person is very rare."

Miss Barry stayed her month and more. Anne kept her in good spirits, and they soon became fast friends.

"Miss Barry is a kindred spirit," Anne said to Marilla. "I didn't realize that right at first. Kindred spirits are not so scarce as I used to think. It's splendid to find out there are so many of them in the world."

Тhe following summer, a new minister and his wife came to Avonlea. Their names were Mr. and Mrs. Allan, and everyone liked them at once. Anne discovered that Mrs. Allan was another kindred spirit, and the two became very good friends.

"I suppose we must have Mr. and Mrs. Allan to tea," said Marilla one day. "Next Wednesday would be good."

"Oh, Marilla, will you let me make a cake for them?" begged Anne. "I'd love to do something for Mrs. Allan."

"You may make a layer cake," Marilla promised.

As Marilla and Anne got the house ready for their visitors, Anne was wild with excitement. But she worried that her cake would not be any good. Her efforts at cooking had a way of turning into disasters, for Anne often became so lost in daydreams that she forgot what she was doing. Anne was so concerned, she dreamed she was being chased by a terrible goblin with a big layer cake for a head!

Wednesday morning came at last. Anne got up very early. She had caught a bad cold, but nothing could have stopped her from making her layer cake.

When she finally shut the oven door upon her creation, she drew a long breath of relief. "I'm sure I didn't forget anything this time," she said to Marilla. And indeed, when the cake was finished, it was as light and feathery as any cake should be. Anne layered it with jelly and imagined Mrs. Allan liking it so much that she asked for a second piece!

The Allans soon arrived, and the tea was a great success. Mrs. Allan complimented Anne on the flowers she had used to decorate the table, and everyone enjoyed the food. At last Anne brought out her cake.

"You must try a piece of this," Marilla said to Mrs. Allan. "Anne made it especially for you."

Mrs. Allan cut a plump piece for herself and took a bite. A very peculiar expression crossed her face. But she kept eating and did not say a word.

Marilla, seeing the look on Mrs. Allan's face, hurried to taste the cake herself. "Anne Shirley!" she exclaimed. "What on earth did you put into that cake?"

"Nothing but what the recipe said, Marilla," said Anne. "Isn't it all right?"

"It's simply horrible. Mrs. Allan, don't eat any more. Anne, what flavoring did you use?"

"Only vanilla," said Anne miserably. She ran to the kitchen to get the bottle of vanilla for Marilla to inspect.

Marilla opened the bottle and sniffed it. "Anne, you've flavored that cake with *liniment!*" she cried. "I broke the liniment bottle last week and poured what was left into an empty vanilla bottle. I should have warned you, but couldn't you have smelled it?"

Anne burst into tears. "I couldn't—I had such a cold!" she said, and raced upstairs to cry in her bedroom.

Soon Anne heard someone enter the room. "Oh, Marilla," Anne said without looking up, "I'm disgraced forever. Everyone in Avonlea will hear that I flavored a cake with liniment. Gilbert—I mean, the boys at school—will never stop laughing at me. Please, don't make me go downstairs until after the Allans have gone home. Maybe Mrs. Allan thinks I tried to poison her. Will you tell her that I didn't mean her any harm?"

"Suppose you tell her so yourself," said a merry voice.

Anne leaped to her feet and saw Mrs. Allan standing there, smiling at her.

"My dear girl, you mustn't cry so," she said. "It's just a funny mistake that anybody might make."

"Oh no, it takes me to make such a mistake," said Anne. "I wanted to have that cake so nice for you, Mrs. Allan."

"I know you did, dear, and I appreciate that just as much as if the cake had turned out right. Now, won't you show me around your flower garden? I'm very interested in flowers."

Anne permitted herself to be led downstairs. Nothing more was said about the liniment cake. After the Allans had left, Anne realized she had enjoyed the day, in spite of the disaster. Still, she said to Marilla, "Isn't it nice to think that tomorrow is a new day with no mistakes in it yet?"

Avonlea had a new teacher when school began in September. Her name was Miss Stacy, and she became another helpful friend to Anne. All of the pupils loved Miss Stacy, for she was a very cheerful and sympathetic young woman. But none blossomed as much under her care as Anne did. She talked about school constantly to Matthew and Marilla, and delighted in telling them all the new things she was learning.

Anne kept busy outside of school as well. One day, she and Diana, along with their friends Ruby Gillis and Jane Andrews, were playing on Barry's Pond with a rowboat that belonged to Diana's father. They decided to act out part of the legend of King Arthur, where a girl named Elaine died for love of a knight, and her body floated down the river on a boat.

It was decided that Anne should play Elaine. She lay down in the rowboat, and the other girls pushed the boat into the pond. They knew it would float across the pond and under a bridge, and finally wash up on the shore farther down. Diana, Ruby, and Jane hurried over to the opposite shore to wait for Anne's arrival.

For a few minutes, Anne drifted along dreamily. She enjoyed pretending she was the heroine of the romantic and tragic tale. Then something happened that was not at all romantic. The boat began to leak!

Anne sat up quickly and stared at the big crack at the bottom of the boat. The boat must have scraped against a stake when it was pushed off the dock, she realized as she watched the water pouring in. What should she do? She did not know how to swim, and there was no way the boat would reach shore before it sank.

Then Anne thought of a solution. When the boat drifted under the bridge, she would climb out and cling to one of the piles until somebody came to rescue her.

And that is just what Anne did. She scrambled up one

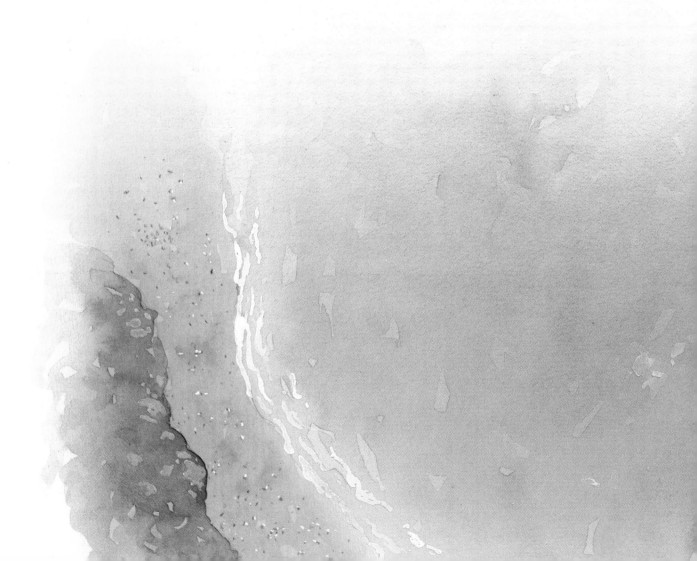

of the piles as quickly as she could, and clung there, wet and shivering. The boat drifted under the bridge and promptly sank. Ruby, Jane, and Diana saw it disappear and thought that Anne had gone down with it. Shrieking at the tops of their voices, they ran back to the house. If they had looked under the bridge, they would have seen Anne there, holding on for dear life. But they did not even glance her way.

The minutes passed by, each one seeming like an hour to the unfortunate Anne. She began to imagine that no one would ever come to rescue her. Suppose she lost her hold on the bridge and slipped down into the watery depths!

Then, just as she thought she could not hold on for another moment, Gilbert Blythe rowed under the bridge in a borrowed boat.

"Anne Shirley, how on earth did you get there?" Gilbert exclaimed. He steered his boat close to the pile and held out a hand. There was nothing for Anne to do but take it and scramble into the boat. She found it very hard to be dignified under the circumstances.

"What happened, Anne?" Gilbert asked as he rowed to shore.

Anne explained her misadventure in a cool voice, not even bothering to look at her rescuer. "I'm much obliged to you," she said when they reached the dock. She jumped out and turned away from Gilbert, but he laid a hand on her arm.

"Anne," he said quickly, "can't we be friends? I'm sorry I made fun of your hair that time. Besides, that was so long ago. I think your hair is very pretty now. Let's be friends."

For an instant, Anne hesitated. The half-shy, half-eager expression in Gilbert's eyes was good to see. But she could not forget her humiliation. She could never forgive him!

"No," she said coldly. "I shall never be friends with you, Gilbert Blythe."

"All right!" Gilbert jumped back into the boat, his cheeks flushed with anger. "I'll never ask you to be friends again, Anne Shirley!" He rowed away with swift strokes.

Anne walked up the path to find her friends and let them know she was all right. She held her head very high, but she could not ignore an odd feeling of regret. She almost wished she had answered Gilbert differently—but it was too late for that now.

Anne was almost fourteen now, and she was one of Miss Stacy's advanced students. One day, Marilla had important news for her. "Miss Stacy came by today while you were out," she told Anne as they sat before the fire. "She wants to organize a special class for students who want to study for the entrance examination to Queen's Academy. Would you like to go to Queen's and study to be a teacher, Anne?"

"Oh, Marilla, I'd love to be a teacher!" Anne cried, clasping her hands in delight. "It's one of my dreams. But won't it be dreadfully expensive?"

"You needn't worry about that part of it. Matthew and I decided when we took you in that we would do the best we could for you. We've put some money aside, so you can join the Queen's class if you like."

Anne did join the class, and she studied harder than ever. The students remained after school for special lessons. Diana did not join the class, and Anne hated to see her leaving school with the others to walk home alone. She and Anne had always walked home from school together. But the Queen's class was very interesting, and it kept Anne busy.

Gilbert was in the class with Anne. The rivalry between them was stronger than ever. Since the day on the pond when Anne refused his offer of friendship, Gilbert ignored her completely. He teased the other girls, and sometimes walked home with one or the other, but he never spoke to Anne. She told herself she did not care—but deep in her heart, she did care, a great deal.

June came, and with it the entrance examination for Queen's. The exams took three days and were held in Charlottetown. Anne stayed with Diana's Aunt Josephine, and worked hard on all her tests. She felt she had done pretty well on everything but geometry. Anne had never had much luck with geometry, and was afraid she hadn't even passed that exam.

Every day, Anne and Diana went to the post office and looked through the Charlottetown newspapers, hoping the pass list would be printed. Anne wanted very much to "pass high." She wanted to come out ahead of Gilbert Blythe, of course. But she also wanted to do well for Matthew and Marilla. She wanted so much for them to be proud of her.

The waiting was unbearable. Finally, three weeks later, the news came. Anne was sitting at her open window when she saw Diana racing down the path, waving a newspaper in her hand.

"Anne, you've passed," Diana cried breathlessly as soon as she burst into Anne's room, "passed the *very first*—you and Gilbert both—you're ties—but your name is first. Oh, I'm so proud!"

Anne snatched up the paper. Yes—there was her name at the very top of a list of two hundred! That moment was worth living for.

"All of Miss Stacy's class passed," Diana told her. "Won't she be delighted?"

Anne ran out into the yard to tell Matthew and Marilla the news. "Well now, I always said it," said Matthew, gazing at the pass list delightedly. "I knew you could beat them all easy."

"You've done pretty well, I must say, Anne," said Marilla, trying to hide her extreme pride.

But Mrs. Lynde, who was also there, was not shy about showing her feelings. "You're a credit to your friends, Anne," she said, "and we're all proud of you."

Things were busy at Green Gables that summer, for there was a lot to do to get Anne ready for Queen's. Leaving Matthew and Marilla was hard. But Anne would be coming home every weekend as long as the weather was good, so she would be seeing them again soon.

The first few days at the Academy were a whirl of excitement. There were new students and teachers to meet, and a lot of studying to do.

Anne made many new friends at Queen's. Her best friends were Stella Maynard and Priscilla Grant. But no one was as dear to her as Diana, home in Avonlea.

Although it usually took two years to get a teacher's license, Anne and Gilbert intended to do it in one year. This meant they would have to work very hard.

In addition, Anne and Gilbert were both competing for the gold medal that was given out every year to the best student. And Anne had her heart set on an Avery scholarship. This was given to the student who had the highest mark in English, and the award was a full scholarship to Redmond College.

"I'll win that scholarship if hard work can do it," Anne decided. "Wouldn't Matthew be proud if I graduated from college? Oh, it's delightful to have ambitions. It makes life so interesting!"

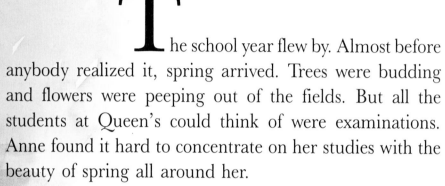

The school year flew by. Almost before anybody realized it, spring arrived. Trees were budding and flowers were peeping out of the fields. But all the students at Queen's could think of were examinations. Anne found it hard to concentrate on her studies with the beauty of spring all around her.

At last, exams were over. On the day the results were posted on the bulletin board, Anne walked to school with her friend, Jane Andrews. Anne was very nervous and pale. In just a few minutes she would know who had won the gold medal and the Avery scholarship. She didn't think she could bear the disappointment if she lost.

As the girls walked up the steps to Queen's, they found the front hall full of boys carrying Gilbert Blythe around on their shoulders. "Hurrah for Blythe, winner of the medal!" they were shouting.

Anne felt a terrible pang of disappointment. Gilbert had beaten her!

And then— "Three cheers for Miss Shirley, winner of the Avery!"

"Oh, Anne," gasped Jane, "I'm so proud of you! Isn't it splendid?"

"I must write home right away," Anne whispered as a group of girls gathered around to congratulate her. "Matthew and Marilla will be so pleased!"

After graduation, Anne went home to Avonlea. She meant to spend the summer visiting with Diana and her other friends, and she would be very busy getting ready to go to Redmond in the fall.

Anne thought Gilbert would be going to Redmond, too. Then Diana told her that he had been offered the job of teaching at the Avonlea school. Anne was very disappointed. College would not be half as much fun without her rival to compete with.

One morning, Anne noticed that Matthew was not looking well. She asked Marilla if anything was wrong.

"No, he's not well at all," Marilla told her. "He had some bad spells with his heart this spring. I've been real worried about him. Maybe now that you're home, he'll be better. You always cheer him up."

Anne took Marilla's hands in her own. "You're not looking well either," she told the old lady. "You must let me do the work this summer while you rest."

Marilla smiled affectionately at Anne. "It's not the work, it's my head. I've got a terrible pain behind my eyes. There's an eye specialist coming to town at the end of June, and I'm going to see him."

That evening, Anne went with Matthew to bring in the cows. "You've been working too hard today," she scolded him. "Why don't you take things easier?"

"Well now, I can't seem to," said Matthew. "I've always worked hard."

"If I'd been the boy you sent for, I'd be able to help you."

"Well now, I'd rather have you than a dozen boys, Anne," said Matthew, patting her hand. "I guess it wasn't a boy that took the Avery scholarship, was it? It was a girl—my girl—my girl that I'm proud of."

He smiled his shy smile at her as he went into the yard. Anne took the memory of that smile with her when she went to her room that night. It would remain with her for a long time.

Matthew—Matthew—what's the matter? Matthew, are you sick?''

Anne heard Marilla's worried cry as she came into the house the next morning, and she ran to see what was wrong. Matthew was standing in the doorway, his face strangely drawn and gray. Before either Marilla or Anne could reach him, he fell across the threshold.

Anne rushed to send the hired man for the doctor, but it was too late. Matthew's heart had given out on him at last.

For Anne, that day passed slowly. There was a terrible ache inside her, and she could not find the tears to release it. It wasn't until the middle of the night that Anne was finally able to weep. Then she could not seem to stop.

Marilla crept in to comfort her. ''Oh, Marilla,'' Anne asked through her tears, ''what will we do without him?''

''We've got each other, Anne. I don't know what I'd do if you weren't here. Oh, Anne, I know I've been strict with you, but you mustn't think I love you any less than Matthew did. I love you as dear as if you were my own flesh and blood, and you've been my joy and comfort ever since you came to Green Gables.''

Matthew was buried two days later. Slowly, life at Green Gables returned to normal. At the end of June, Marilla went into town to see the eye doctor. She was very dejected when she came home.

"The doctor says that I must give up reading and sewing altogether," she told Anne. "If I don't, I'll go completely blind!"

Anne was horrified, but she said bravely, "If you are careful, you won't lose your sight."

"What am I to live for if I can't read or sew or do the work around here?" Marilla answered. "But there, it's no good talking about it."

After Marilla went to bed, Anne sat in her window and cried. How sadly things had changed since she had come home from Queen's! But by the time Anne got into bed, there was a smile on her face and peace in her heart. She had made a decision.

A few days later, Marilla told Anne she was thinking of selling Green Gables. "I hate to do it, but I don't know what else there is to be done," Marilla said. "If my eyes were strong, I could manage here with a hired man, but I can't do the work anymore. I'm sorry you won't have a home to come to on your vacations from college, Anne, but that's the way it will have to be."

"You mustn't sell Green Gables," Anne said firmly.

"I have to. I can't stay here alone. I'd go crazy with loneliness."

"You won't be alone, Marilla. I'll be here with you. I'm not going to Redmond."

"Not going to Redmond!" Marilla cried in astonishment. "What do you mean?"

"Just what I say. I decided not to go the night you came home from the doctor's. How could I leave you alone with such trouble, after all you've done for me? I've been thinking and planning," Anne continued. "Mr. Barry wants to rent the farm next year, so you don't have to worry about the work. And I'm going to teach. I've applied for the school here, but I've heard it's already been promised to Gilbert Blythe. But I can have the school in Carmody. I'll drive the buggy back and forth until winter, and even then, I could come home most weekends. We'll be real cozy and happy here together, you and I."

"Oh, Anne, I could get on real well if you were here. But I can't let you sacrifice yourself for me."

"Nonsense!" Anne said with a laugh. "There's no sacrifice. I'm as ambitious as ever, you know. I've just changed the object of my ambitions. I'm going to be a good teacher. I shall give life here my best, and I believe it will give its best to me in return."

Anne looked into Marilla's tired, but joyful, face. "When I left Queen's, my future seemed to stretch out before me like a straight road. I thought I could see along it for a long way. Now there's a bend in the road. I don't know what lies beyond that bend, but I'm going to believe that the best waits for me there."

Mrs. Lynde wholeheartedly approved of Anne's staying at Green Gables. One evening, when she had come up for a visit, she said, "I guess you're going to be teaching right here in Avonlea, Anne. It's been decided that you're to have the school."

Anne jumped to her feet in surprise. "But I thought it had already been promised to Gilbert Blythe!" she said.

"So it had. But as soon as Gilbert heard you had applied for it, he withdrew his application. He's going to teach at White Sands instead. Of course, he gave up the school just to oblige you. Wasn't that real kind and thoughtful of him?"

"I don't feel that I ought to take it," murmured Anne. "I can't let Gilbert make such a sacrifice for me."

"You can't stop him now. He's already signed the papers at White Sands. The Avonlea school is yours."

The next evening, Anne went to the little Avonlea graveyard to put fresh flowers on Matthew's grave. As she walked home, she met Gilbert on the road. He lifted his cap to her politely, but would have passed by in silence if Anne had not stopped and held out her hand.

"Gilbert," she said, her cheeks bright red, "I want to thank you for giving up the school for me."

Gilbert took her hand eagerly. "I was pleased to be able to do you some small service," he said. "Are we going to be friends now? Have you forgiven me at last?"

Anne laughed. "I forgave you that day by the pond, although I didn't know it. I've been sorry ever since."

"We are going to be the very best of friends," Gilbert declared joyfully. "We were born to be good friends. Come, I'm going to walk you home."

Anne and Gilbert stood by Anne's gate for half an hour, talking. After all, as Anne told Marilla later, they had five years' lost conversation to catch up on.

Anne sat for a long time at her window that night. The wind purred softly in the trees, and the stars twinkled cheerfully over the fields.

Anne knew the road before her had narrowed since the night she came home from Queen's. But she also knew there would be flowers of quiet happiness along the path. Nothing could rob her of her world of dreams, or of the joys of work and friendship. And there was always the bend in the road!

"All's right with the world," Anne whispered softly.